Bartleby, the Scrivener

Bartleby, the Scrivener: A Story of Wall Street
by Herman Melville

This edition has been published in 2019 in the United Kingdom
by Paper + Ink.

www.paperand.ink
Twitter: @paper_andink
Instagram: paper_and.ink
Facebook: https://www.facebook.com/paperwithink/
Patreon: https://www.patreon.com/paper_ink

This novella was first serialized anonymously in two parts in the
November and December 1853 issues of *Putnam's Monthly Magazine of
American Literature, Science and Art*.
Minor changes to punctuation, spelling and formatting have been made.

1 2 3 4 5 6 7 8 9 10

ISBN 9781911475217

A CIP catalogue record for this book is available from the British Library.
Jacket design by James Nunn: www.jamesnunn.co.uk | @Jamesnunnart
Printed and bound in Poland by Opolgraf: www.opolgraf.com

Bartleby, the Scrivener
Herman Melville

BARTLEBY, THE SCRIVENER

A Story of Wall Street

I am a rather elderly man. The nature of my avocations for the last thirty years has brought me into more than ordinary contact with what would seem an interesting and somewhat singular set of men, of whom as yet nothing that I know of has ever been written: I mean the law-copyists, or scriveners. I have known very many of them, professionally and privately, and if I pleased, could relate divers histories, at which good-natured gentlemen might smile and sentimental souls might weep. But I waive the biographies of all other scriveners for a few passages in the life of Bartleby, who was a scrivener the strangest I ever saw or heard of.

While of other law-copyists I might write the complete life, of Bartleby nothing of that sort can be done. I believe that no materials exist for a full and satisfactory biography of this man. It is an irreparable loss to literature. Bartleby was one of those beings of whom nothing is ascertainable, except from the original sources, and in his case those are very small. What my own astonished eyes saw of Bartleby, that is all I know of him, except, indeed, one vague report, which will appear in the sequel.

Ere introducing the scrivener as he first appeared to me, it is fit I make some mention of myself, my employees, my business, my chambers and general surroundings; because some such description is indispensable to an adequate understanding of the chief character about to be presented.

Imprimis: I am a man who, from his youth upwards, has been filled with a profound conviction that the easiest way of life is the best. Hence, though I belong to a profession proverbially energetic and nervous – even to turbulence, at times – yet nothing of that sort have I ever suffered to invade my peace. I am one of those unambitious lawyers who never addresses a jury, or in any way draws down public applause; but in the cool tranquillity of a snug retreat, do a snug business among rich men's bonds and mortgages and title deeds. All who know me consider me an eminently safe man. The late John Jacob Astor, a personage little given to poetic enthusiasm, had no hesitation in pronouncing my first grand point to be prudence; my next, method. I do not speak it in vanity, but simply record the fact, that I was not unemployed in my profession by the late John Jacob Astor; a name which, I admit, I love to repeat, for it hath a rounded and orbicular sound to it, and rings like unto bullion. I will freely add that I was not insensible to the late John Jacob Astor's good opinion.

Some time prior to the period at which this little history begins, my avocations had been largely increased. The good old office, now extinct in the State of New York, of a Master in Chancery, had been conferred upon me. It was not a very arduous office, but very pleasantly remunerative. I seldom lose my temper, much more seldom indulge in dangerous indignation at wrongs and outrages; but I must be permitted to be rash here and declare that I consider the sudden and violent abrogation of the office of Master of Chancery by the new Constitution as a ... premature act; inasmuch as I had counted upon a life-lease of the profits, whereas I only received those of a few short years. But this is by the way.

My chambers were up stairs at No. — Wall Street. At one end, they looked upon the white wall of the interior of a spacious skylight shaft, penetrating the building from top to bottom. This view might have been considered rather tame than otherwise, deficient in what landscape painters call 'life'. But if so, the view from the other end of my chambers offered, at least, a contrast, if nothing more. In that direction my windows commanded an unobstructed view of a lofty brick wall, black by age and everlasting shade; which wall required no spy-glass to bring out its lurking beauties, but for the benefit of all nearsighted spectators, was pushed up to within ten feet of my window panes. Owing to the great height of the surrounding buildings, and my chambers being on the second floor, the interval between this wall and mine not a little resembled a huge square cistern.

At the period just preceding the advent of Bartleby, I had two persons as copyists in my employment, and a promising lad as an office boy. First, Turkey; second, Nippers; third, Ginger Nut. These may seem names, the like of which are not usually found in the Directory. In truth, they were nicknames, mutually conferred upon each other by my three clerks, and were deemed expressive of their respective persons or characters. Turkey was a short, pursy Englishman of about my own age, that is, somewhere not far from sixty. In the morning, one might say, his face was of a fine florid hue, but after twelve o'clock, meridian – his dinner hour – it blazed like a grate full of Christmas coals, and continued blazing – but, as it were, with a gradual wane – till six o'clock PM or thereabouts, after which I saw no more of the proprietor of the face, which gaining its meridian with the sun seemed to set with it, to rise, culminate and decline the following day, with the like regularity and undiminished glory. There are many singular coincidences I have known in the course of my life, not the least among which was the fact that exactly when Turkey displayed his fullest beams from his red and radiant countenance, just then, too, at that critical moment, began the daily period when I considered his business capacities as seriously disturbed for the remainder of the twenty-four hours.

Not that he was absolutely idle, or averse to business then; far from it. The difficulty was, he was apt to be altogether too energetic. There was a strange, inflamed, flurried, flighty recklessness of activity about him. He would be incautious in dipping his pen into his inkstand. All his blots upon my documents were dropped there after twelve o'clock, meridian. Indeed, not only would he be reckless and sadly given to making blots in the afternoon, but some days he went further, and was rather noisy. At such times, too, his face flamed with augmented blazonry, as if cannel coal had been heaped on anthracite. He made an unpleasant racket with his chair; spilled his sand-box; in mending his pens, impatiently split them all to pieces and threw them on the floor in a sudden passion; stood up and leaned over his table, boxing his papers about in a most indecorous manner, very sad to behold in an elderly man like him.

Nevertheless, as he was in many ways a most valuable person to me, and all the time before twelve o'clock, meridian, was the quickest, steadiest creature too, accomplishing a great deal of work in a style not easy to be matched – for these reasons, I was willing to overlook his eccentricities, though indeed, occasionally, I remonstrated with him. I did this very gently, however, because, though the civilest, nay, the blandest and most reverential of men in the morning, yet in the afternoon he was disposed, upon provocation, to be slightly rash with his tongue – in fact, insolent. Now, valuing his morning services as I did, and resolved not to lose them, yet at the same time made uncomfortable by his inflamed ways after twelve o'clock, and being a man of peace, unwilling by my admonitions to call forth unseemly retorts from him, I took upon me one Saturday noon (he was always worse on Saturdays) to hint to him – very kindly – that perhaps now that he was growing old, it might be well to abridge his labours; in short, he need not come to my chambers after twelve o'clock, but, dinner over, had best go home to his lodgings and rest himself till tea time. But no; he insisted upon his afternoon devotions. His countenance became intolerably fervid, as he oratorically assured me – gesticulating with a long ruler at the other end of the room – that if his services in the morning were useful, how indispensable, then, in the afternoon?

"With submission, sir," said Turkey on this occasion, "I consider myself your right-hand man. In the morning I but marshal and deploy my columns; but in the afternoon I put myself at their head, and gallantly charge the foe, thus!" (and he made a violent thrust with the ruler).

"But the blots, Turkey," intimated I.

"True, but, with submission, sir, behold these hairs! I am getting old. Surely, sir, a blot or two of a warm afternoon is not to be severely urged against grey hairs. Old age – even if it blot the page – is honourable. With submission, sir, we both are getting old."

This appeal to my fellow-feeling was hardly to be resisted. At all events, I saw that go he would not. So I made up my mind to let him stay, resolving, nevertheless, to see to it that, during the afternoon, he had to do with my less important papers.

Nippers, the second on my list, was a whiskered, sallow and, upon the whole, rather piratical-looking young man of about five and twenty. I always deemed him the victim of two evil powers: ambition and indigestion. The ambition was evinced by a certain impatience of the duties of a mere copyist, an unwarrantable usurpation of strictly professional affairs, such as the original drawing up of legal documents. The indigestion seemed betokened in an occasional nervous testiness and grinning irritability, causing the teeth to audibly grind together over mistakes committed in copying; unnecessary maledictions, hissed, rather than spoken, in the heat of business; and especially by a continual discontent with the height of the table where he worked. Though of a very ingenious mechanical turn, Nippers could never get this table to suit him. He put chips under it, blocks of various sorts, bits of pasteboard and, at last, went so far as to attempt an exquisite adjustment by final pieces of folded blotting-paper. But no invention would answer. If, for the sake of easing his back, he brought the table lid at a sharp angle well up toward his chin, and wrote there like a man using the steep roof of a Dutch house for his desk, then he declared that it stopped the circulation in his arms. If now he lowered the table to his waistbands, and stooped over it in writing, then there was a sore aching in his back. In short, the truth of the matter was, Nippers knew not what he wanted. Or, if he wanted any thing, it was to be rid of a scrivener's table altogether.

Among the manifestations of his diseased ambition was a fondness he had for receiving visits from certain ambiguous-looking fellows in seedy coats, whom he called his clients. Indeed, I was aware that not only was he, at times, considerable of a ward politician, but he occasionally did a little business at the Justices' courts, and was not unknown on the steps of the Tombs. I have good reason to believe, however, that one individual who called upon him at my chambers, and who, with a grand air, he insisted was his client, was no other than a dun – and the alleged title-deed, a bill. But with all his failings, and the annoyances he caused me, Nippers, like his compatriot Turkey, was a very useful man to me; wrote a neat, swift hand; and, when he chose, was not deficient in a gentlemanly sort of deportment. Added to this, he always dressed in a gentlemanly sort of way, and so, incidentally, reflected credit upon my chambers.

Whereas with respect to Turkey, I had much ado to

keep him from being a reproach to me. His clothes were apt to look oily and smell of eating-houses. He wore his pantaloons very loose and baggy in summer. His coats were execrable; his hat, not be to handled. But while the hat was a thing of indifference to me, inasmuch as his natural civility and deference, as a dependent Englishman, always led him to doff it the moment he entered the room, yet his coat was another matter. Concerning his coats, I reasoned with him, but with no effect. The truth was, I suppose, that a man with so small an income could not afford to sport such a lustrous face and a lustrous coat at one and the same time. As Nippers once observed, Turkey's money went chiefly for red ink. One winter day, I presented Turkey with a highly respectable-looking coat of my own, a padded grey coat of a most comfortable warmth, and which buttoned straight up from the knee to the neck. I thought Turkey would appreciate the favour, and abate his rashness and obstreperousness of afternoons. But no. I verily believe that buttoning himself up in so downy and blanket-like a coat had a pernicious effect upon him; upon the same principle that too much oats are bad for horses. In fact, precisely as a rash, restive horse is said to feel his oats, so Turkey felt his coat. It made him insolent. He was a man whom prosperity harmed.

Though concerning the self-indulgent habits of Turkey I had my own private surmises, yet touching Nippers I was well persuaded that whatever might be his faults in other respects, he was, at least, a temperate young man. But indeed, Nature herself seemed to have been his vintner, and at his birth charged him so thoroughly with an irritable, brandy-like disposition, that all subsequent potations were needless. When I consider how, amid the stillness of my chambers, Nippers would sometimes impatiently rise from his seat, and, stooping over his table, spread his arms wide apart, seize the whole desk, and move it and jerk it with a grim, grinding motion on the floor, as if the table were a perverse voluntary agent intent on thwarting and vexing him, I plainly perceive that for Nippers, brandy and water were altogether superfluous.

It was fortunate for me that, owing to its peculiar cause – indigestion – the irritability and consequent nervousness of Nippers were mainly observable in the morning, while in the afternoon he was comparatively mild. So that Turkey's paroxysms only coming on about twelve o'clock, I never had to do with their eccentricities at one time. Their fits relieved each other like guards. When Nippers's was on, Turkey's was off, and vice versa. This was a good natural arrangement under the circumstances.

Ginger Nut, the third on my list, was a lad some twelve years old. His father was a carman, ambitious of seeing his son on the bench instead of a cart before he died. So he sent him to my office as student-at-law, errand boy and cleaner and sweeper, at the rate of one dollar a week. He had a little desk to himself, but he did not use it much. Upon inspection, the drawer exhibited a great array of the shells of various sorts of nuts. Indeed, to this quick-witted youth, the whole noble science of the law was contained in a nutshell. Not the least among the employments of Ginger Nut, as well as one which he discharged with the most alacrity, was his duty as cake and apple purveyor for Turkey and Nippers. Copying law papers being proverbially a dry, husky sort of business, my two scriveners were fain to moisten their mouths very often with Spitzenbergs to be had at the numerous stalls nigh the Custom House and Post Office. Also, they sent Ginger Nut very frequently for that peculiar cake – small, flat, round and very spicy – after which he had been named by them. Of a cold morning when business was but dull, Turkey would gobble up scores of these cakes, as if they were mere wafers – indeed, they sell them at the rate of six or eight for a penny – the scrape of his pen blending with the crunching of the crisp particles in his mouth. Of all the fiery afternoon blunders and flurried rashnesses of Turkey was his once moistening a ginger cake between his lips and clapping it onto a mortgage for a seal. I came within an ace of dismissing him then. But he mollified me by making an oriental bow, and saying, "With submission, sir, it was generous of me to find you in stationery on my own account."

Now, my original business – that of a conveyancer and title hunter, and drawer-up of recondite documents of all sorts – was considerably increased by receiving the master's office. There was now great work for scriveners. Not only must I push the clerks already with me, but I must have additional help. In answer to my advertisement, a motionless young man one morning stood upon my office threshold, the door being open, for it was summer. I can see that figure now –pallidly neat, pitiably respectable, incurably forlorn! It was Bartleby.

After a few words touching his qualifications, I engaged him, glad to have among my corps of copyists a man of so singularly sedate an aspect, which I thought might operate beneficially upon the flighty temper of Turkey and the fiery one of Nippers.

I should have stated before that ground-glass

folding doors divided my premises into two parts, one of which was occupied by my scriveners, the other by myself. According to my humour, I threw open these doors or closed them. I resolved to assign Bartleby a corner by the folding doors, but on my side of them, so as to have this quiet man within easy call, in case any trifling thing was to be done. I placed his desk close up to a small side-window in that part of the room, a window which originally had afforded a lateral view of certain grimy backyards and bricks, but which, owing to subsequent erections, commanded at present no view at all, though it gave some light. Within three feet of the panes was a wall, and the light came down from far above, between two lofty buildings, as from a very small opening in a dome. Still further to a satisfactory arrangement, I procured a high green folding screen, which might entirely isolate Bartleby from my sight, though not remove him from my voice. And thus, in a manner, privacy and society were conjoined.

At first, Bartleby did an extraordinary quantity of writing. As if long famishing for something to copy, he seemed to gorge himself on my documents. There was no pause for digestion. He ran a day and night line, copying by sunlight and by candlelight. I should have been quite delighted with his application, had be been cheerfully industrious. But he wrote on silently, palely, mechanically.

It is, of course, an indispensable part of a scrivener's business to verify the accuracy of his copy, word by word. Where there are two or more scriveners in an office, they assist each other in this examination, one reading from the copy, the other holding the original. It is a very dull, wearisome and lethargic affair. I can readily imagine that to some sanguine temperaments it would be altogether intolerable. For example, I cannot credit that the mettlesome poet Byron would have contentedly sat down with Bartleby to examine a law document of, say five hundred pages, closely written in a crimpy hand.

Now and then, in the haste of business, it had been my habit to assist in comparing some brief document myself, calling Turkey or Nippers for this purpose. One object I had in placing Bartleby so handy to me behind the screen was to avail myself of his services on such trivial occasions. It was on the third day, I think, of his being with me, and before any necessity had arisen for having his own writing examined, that, being much hurried to complete a small affair I had in hand, I abruptly called to Bartleby. In my haste and natural expectancy of instant compliance, I sat with my head bent over the original on my desk, and my right hand sideways and somewhat nervously extended with the copy, so that immediately upon emerging from his retreat, Bartleby might snatch it and proceed to business without the least delay.

In this very attitude did I sit when I called to him, rapidly stating what it was I wanted him to do – namely, to examine a small paper with me. Imagine my surprise, nay, my consternation, when, without moving from his privacy, Bartleby in a singularly mild, firm voice, replied: "I would prefer not to."

I sat awhile in perfect silence, rallying my stunned faculties. Immediately it occurred to me that my ears had deceived me, or Bartleby had entirely misunderstood my meaning. I repeated my request in the clearest tone I could assume. But in quite as clear a one came the previous reply: "I would prefer not to."

"'Prefer not to'!" echoed I, rising in high excitement and crossing the room with a stride. "What do you mean? Are you moonstruck? I want you to help me compare this sheet here – take it," and I thrust it toward him.

"I would prefer not to," said he.

I looked at him steadfastly. His face was leanly composed; his grey eye dimly calm. Not a wrinkle of agitation rippled him. Had there been the least uneasiness, anger, impatience or impertinence in his manner – in other words, had there been anything ordinarily human about him – doubtless I should have violently dismissed him from the premises. But as it was, I should have as soon thought of turning my pale, plaster-of-Paris bust of Cicero out of doors. I stood gazing at him awhile, as he went on with his own writing, and then reseated myself at my desk. *This is very strange,* thought I. What had one best do? But my business hurried me. I concluded to forget the matter for the present, reserving it for my future leisure. So, calling Nippers from the other room, the paper was speedily examined.

A few days after this, Bartleby concluded four lengthy documents, being quadruplicates of a week's testimony taken before me in my High Court of Chancery. It became necessary to examine them. It was an important suit, and great accuracy was imperative. Having all things arranged I called Turkey, Nippers and Ginger Nut from the next room, meaning to place the four copies in the hands of my four clerks while I should read from the original. Accordingly, Turkey, Nippers and Ginger Nut had taken their seats in a row, each with his document in hand, when I called to

Bartleby to join this interesting group.

"Bartleby! Quick, I am waiting."

I heard a slow scrape of his chair legs on the uncarpeted floor, and soon he appeared standing at the entrance of his hermitage.

"What is wanted?" said he, mildly.

"The copies, the copies," said I hurriedly. "We are going to examine them. There" – and I held toward him the fourth quadruplicate.

"I would prefer not to," he said, and gently disappeared behind the screen.

For a few moments I was turned into a pillar of salt, standing at the head of my seated column of clerks. Recovering myself, I advanced toward the screen and demanded the reason for such extraordinary conduct.

"Why do you refuse?"

"I would prefer not to."

With any other man I should have flown outright into a dreadful passion, scorned all further words and thrust him ignominiously from my presence. But there was something about Bartleby that not only strangely disarmed me, but in a wonderful manner touched and disconcerted me.

I began to reason with him.

"These are your own copies we are about to examine.

It is labour-saving to you, because one examination will answer for your four papers. It is common usage. Every copyist is bound to help examine his copy. Is it not so? Will you not speak? Answer!"

"I prefer not to," he replied in a flute-like tone. It seemed to me that while I had been addressing him, he carefully revolved every statement that I made; fully comprehended the meaning; could not gainsay the irresistible conclusion; but, at the same time, some paramount consideration prevailed with him to reply as he did.

"You are decided, then, not to comply with my request – a request made according to common usage and common sense?"

He briefly gave me to understand that on that point my judgment was sound. Yes: his decision was irreversible.

It is not seldom the case that when a man is browbeaten in some unprecedented and violently unreasonable way, he begins to stagger in his own plainest faith. He begins, as it were, vaguely to surmise that, wonderful as it may be, all the justice and all the reason are on the other side. Accordingly, if any disinterested persons are present, he turns to them for some reinforcement for his own faltering mind.

"Turkey," said I, "what do you think of this? Am I not right?"

"With submission, sir," said Turkey with his blandest tone, "I think that you are."

"Nippers," said I, "what do you think of it?"

"I think I should kick him out of the office."

(The reader of nice perceptions will here perceive that, it being morning, Turkey's answer is couched in polite and tranquil terms, but Nippers replies in ill-tempered ones. Or, to repeat a previous sentence, Nippers's ugly mood was on duty, and Turkey's off.)

"Ginger Nut," said I, willing to enlist the smallest suffrage in my behalf, "what do you think of it?"

"I think, sir, he's a little loony," replied Ginger Nut, with a grin.

"You hear what they say," said I, turning toward the screen, "come forth and do your duty."

But he vouchsafed no reply. I pondered a moment in sore perplexity. But once more, business hurried me. I determined again to postpone the consideration of this dilemma to my future leisure. With a little trouble, we made out to examine the papers without Bartleby, though at every page or two, Turkey deferentially dropped his opinion that this proceeding was quite out of the common; while Nippers, twitching in his chair with a dyspeptic nervousness, ground out between his set teeth occasional hissing maledictions against the stubborn oaf behind the screen. And for his (Nippers's) part, this was the first and the last time he would do another man's business without pay. Meanwhile, Bartleby sat in his hermitage, oblivious to every thing but his own peculiar business there.

Some days passed, the scrivener being employed upon another lengthy work. His late remarkable conduct led me to regard his ways narrowly. I observed that he never went to dinner; indeed, that he never went anywhere. As yet I had never, of my personal knowledge, known him to be outside of my office. He was a perpetual sentry in the corner. At about eleven o'clock, though, in the morning, I noticed that Ginger Nut would advance toward the opening in Bartleby's screen, as if silently beckoned thither by a gesture invisible to me where I sat. The boy would then leave the office, jingling a few pence, and reappear with a handful of ginger nuts which he delivered in the hermitage, receiving two of the cakes for his trouble.

He lives, then, on ginger nuts, thought I; never eats a dinner, properly speaking; he must be a vegetarian, then. But no – he never eats even vegetables; he eats nothing but ginger nuts. My mind then ran on in reveries concerning the probable effects upon the human constitution of living entirely on ginger nuts. Ginger nuts are so called because they contain ginger as one of their peculiar constituents, and the final flavouring one. Now what was ginger? A hot, spicy thing. Was Bartleby hot and spicy? Not at all. Ginger, then, had no effect upon Bartleby. Probably he preferred it should have none.

Nothing so aggravates an earnest person as a passive resistance. If the individual so resisted be of a not inhumane temper, and the resisting one perfectly harmless in his passivity; then, in the better moods of the former, he will endeavour charitably to construe to his imagination what proves impossible to be solved by his judgment. Even so, for the most part, I regarded Bartleby and his ways. *Poor fellow!* thought I, *he means no mischief; it is plain he intends no insolence; his aspect sufficiently evinces that his eccentricities are involuntary. He is useful to me. I can get along with him. If I turn him away, the chances are he will fall in with some less indulgent employer, and then he will be rudely treated and perhaps driven forth miserably to starve. Yes. Here I can cheaply purchase a delicious self-approval. To befriend Bartleby, to humour him in his strange wilfulness, will cost me little or nothing, while*

I lay up in my soul what will eventually prove a sweet morsel for my conscience.

But this mood was not invariable with me. The passiveness of Bartleby sometimes irritated me. I felt strangely goaded on to encounter him in new opposition, to elicit some angry spark from him answerable to my own. But indeed, I might as well have essayed to strike fire with my knuckles against a bit of Windsor soap. But one afternoon, the evil impulse in me mastered me, and the following little scene ensued:

"Bartleby," said I, "when those papers are all copied, I will compare them with you."

"I would prefer not to."

"How? Surely you do not mean to persist in that mulish vagary?"

No answer.

I threw open the folding doors nearby, and, turning upon Turkey and Nippers,   exclaimed   in   an excited manner: "He says, a second time, he won't examine his papers. What do you think of it, Turkey?"

It was afternoon, be it remembered. Turkey sat glowing like a brass boiler, his bald head steaming, his hands reeling among his blotted papers.

"Think of it?" roared Turkey; "I think I'll just step behind his screen, and black his eyes for him!"

So saying, Turkey rose to his feet and threw his arms into a pugilistic position. He was hurrying away to make good his promise when I detained him, alarmed at the effect of incautiously rousing Turkey's combativeness after dinner.

"Sit down, Turkey," said I, "and hear what Nippers has to say. What do you think of it, Nippers? Would I not be justified in immediately dismissing Bartleby?"

"Excuse me, that is for you to decide, sir. I think his conduct quite unusual, and indeed unjust, as regards Turkey and myself. But it may only be a passing whim."

"Ah," exclaimed I, "you have strangely changed your mind then – you speak very gently of him now."

"All beer," cried Turkey, "gentleness is effects of beer – Nippers and I dined together today. You see how gentle I am, sir. Shall I go and black his eyes?"

"You refer to Bartleby, I suppose. No, not today, Turkey," I replied. "Pray, put up your fists." I closed the doors and again advanced toward Bartleby. I felt additional incentives tempting me to my fate. I burned to be rebelled against again. I remembered that Bartleby never left the office.

"Bartleby," said I, "Ginger Nut is away; just step round to the Post Office, won't you?" – it was but three minutes' walk – "and see if there is anything for me."

"I would prefer not to."

"You will not?"

"I prefer not."

I staggered to my desk and sat there in a deep study. My blind inveteracy returned. Was there any other thing in which I could procure myself to be ignominiously repulsed by this lean, penniless wight, my hired clerk? What added thing is there, perfectly reasonable, that he will be sure to refuse to do?

"Bartleby!"

No answer.

"Bartleby!" in a louder tone.

No answer.

"Bartleby!" I roared.

Like a very ghost, agreeably to the laws of magical invocation, at the third summons he appeared at the entrance of his hermitage.

"Go to the next room and tell Nippers to come to me."

"I prefer not to," he respectfully and slowly said, and mildly disappeared.

"Very good, Bartleby," said I, in a quiet sort of serenely severe, self-possessed tone, intimating the unalterable purpose of some terrible retribution very close at hand. At the moment, I half-intended something of the kind. But upon the whole, as it was drawing toward my dinner-hour, I thought it best to put on my hat and walk home for the day, suffering much from perplexity and distress of mind.

Shall I acknowledge it? The conclusion of this whole business was that it soon became a fixed fact of my chambers that a pale young scrivener by the name of Bartleby had a desk there; that he copied for me at the usual rate of four cents a folio (one hundred words); but that he was permanently exempt from examining the work done by him, such duty being transferred to Turkey and Nippers, one of compliment doubtless to their superior acuteness; moreover, said Bartleby was never on any account to be dispatched on the most trivial errand of any sort; and that, even if entreated to take upon him such a matter, it was generally understood that he would *prefer not to*: in other words, that he would refuse, point-blank.

As days passed on, I became considerably reconciled to Bartleby. His steadiness, his freedom from all dissipation, his incessant industry (except when he chose to throw himself into a standing reverie behind his screen), his great stillness, his unalterableness of demeanour under all circumstances, made him a valuable acquisition. One prime thing was this: he was always there, first in the morning, continually through the day and the last at night. I had a singular confidence in his honesty. I felt my most precious papers perfectly safe in his hands. Sometimes, to be sure, I could not, for the very soul of me, avoid falling into sudden spasmodic passions with him. For it was exceedingly difficult to bear in mind all the time those strange peculiarities, privileges and unheard-of exemptions forming the tacit stipulations on Bartleby's part under which he remained in my office. Now and then, in the eagerness of dispatching pressing business, I would inadvertently summon Bartleby in a short, rapid tone, to put his finger, say, on the incipient tie of a bit of red tape with which I was about compressing some papers. Of course, from behind the screen the usual answer, *"I prefer not to"*, was sure to come; and then, how could a human creature with the common infirmities of our nature refrain from bitterly exclaiming upon such perverseness – such unreasonableness! However, every added repulse of this sort which I received only tended to lessen the probability of my repeating the inadvertence.

Here it must be said that, according to the custom of most legal gentlemen occupying chambers in densely populated law buildings, there were several keys to my door. One was kept by a woman residing in the attic, which person weekly scrubbed and daily swept and dusted my apartments. Another was kept by Turkey, for convenience's sake. The third I sometimes carried in my own pocket. The fourth I knew not who had.

Now, one Sunday morning I happened to go to Trinity Church to hear a celebrated preacher and, finding myself rather early on the ground, I thought I would walk round to my chambers for a while. Luckily I had my key with me; but upon applying it to the lock, I found it resisted by something inserted from the inside. Quite surprised, I called out; when, to my consternation, a key was turned from within, and, thrusting his lean visage at me and holding the door ajar, the apparition of Bartleby appeared, in his shirtsleeves, and otherwise in a strangely tattered dishabille, saying quietly that he was sorry, but he was deeply engaged just then, and preferred not admitting me at present. In a brief word or two, he moreover added, perhaps I had better walk round the block two or three times, and by that time he would probably have concluded his affairs.

Now, the utterly unsurmised appearance of Bartleby, tenanting my law chambers of a Sunday morning, with his cadaverously gentlemanly nonchalance, yet withal firm and self-possessed, had such a strange effect upon me that, incontinently, I slunk away from my own door and did as desired. But not without sundry twinges of impotent rebellion against the mild effrontery of this unaccountable scrivener. Indeed, it was his wonderful mildness, chiefly, which not only disarmed me but unmanned me, as it were. For I consider that one, for the time, is a sort of unmanned when he tranquilly permits his hired clerk to dictate to him and order him away from his own premises.

Furthermore, I was full of uneasiness as to what Bartleby could possibly be doing in my office in his shirtsleeves, and in an otherwise dismantled condition of a Sunday morning. Was anything amiss going on? Nay, that was out of the question. It was not to be thought of for a moment that Bartleby was an immoral person. But what could he be doing there? Copying? Nay again; whatever might be his eccentricities, Bartleby was an eminently decorous person. He would be the last man to sit down to his desk in any state approaching to nudity. Besides, it was Sunday; and there was something about Bartleby that forbade the supposition that we would by any secular occupation violate the proprieties of the day.

Nevertheless, my mind was not pacified; and full of a

restless curiosity, at last I returned to the door. Without hindrance I inserted my key, opened it and entered. Bartleby was not to be seen. I looked round anxiously, peeped behind his screen; but it was very plain that he was gone. Upon more closely examining the place, I surmised that for an indefinite period Bartleby must have ate, dressed and slept in my office, and that, too, without plate, mirror or bed. The cushioned seat of a rickety old sofa in one corner bore the faint impress of a lean, reclining form. Rolled away under his desk, I found a blanket; under the empty grate, a blacking box and brush; on a chair, a tin basin with soap and a ragged towel; in a newspaper, a few crumbs of ginger nuts and a morsel of cheese.

Yet, thought I, it is evident enough that Bartleby has been making his home here, keeping bachelor's hall all by himself. Immediately then, the thought came sweeping across me: what miserable friendlessness and loneliness are here revealed! His poverty is great, but his solitude, how horrible! Think of it. Of a Sunday, Wall Street is as deserted as Petra; and every night of every day, it is an emptiness. This building, too, which of weekdays hums with industry and life, at nightfall echoes with sheer vacancy, and all through Sunday is forlorn. And here Bartleby makes his home, sole spectator of a solitude which he has seen all populous – a sort of innocent and transformed Marius brooding among the ruins of Carthage!

For the first time in my life, a feeling of overpowering, stinging melancholy seized me. Before, I had never experienced aught but a not-unpleasing sadness. The bond of a common humanity now drew me irresistibly to gloom. A fraternal melancholy! For both I and Bartleby were sons of Adam. I remembered the bright silks and sparkling faces I had seen that day, in gala trim, swan-like, sailing down the Mississippi of Broadway; and I contrasted them with the pallid copyist, and thought to myself: *Ah, happiness courts the light, so we deem the world is gay; but misery hides aloof, so we deem that misery there is none.* These sad fancyings – chimeras, doubtless, of a sick and silly brain – led on to other and more special thoughts concerning the eccentricities of Bartleby. Presentiments of strange discoveries hovered round me. The scrivener's pale form appeared to me laid out, among uncaring strangers, in its shivering, winding sheet.

Suddenly, I was attracted by Bartleby's closed desk, the key in open sight left in the lock. I mean no mischief, seek the gratification of no heartless curiosity, thought I; besides, the desk is mine, and its contents, too, so I will make bold to look within. Everything was methodically arranged, the papers smoothly placed. The pigeonholes were deep, and removing the files of documents, I groped into their recesses. Presently I felt something there, and dragged it out. It was an old bandanna handkerchief, heavy and knotted. I opened it, and saw it was a savings bank.

I now recalled all the quiet mysteries that I had noted in the man. I remembered that he never spoke but to answer; that, though at intervals he had considerable time to himself, yet I had never seen him reading – no, not even a newspaper; that, for long periods, he would stand looking out, at his pale window behind the screen, upon the dead brick wall; I was quite sure he never visited any refectory or eating house, while his pale face clearly indicated that he never drank beer like Turkey, or tea and coffee even, like other men; that he never went anywhere in particular that I could learn; never went out for a walk, unless, indeed, that was the case at present; that he had declined telling who he was or whence he came, or whether he had any relatives in the world; that, though so thin and pale, he never complained of ill health. And more than all, I remembered a certain unconscious air of pallid – how shall I call it? – of pallid haughtiness, say, or rather, an austere reserve about him, which had positively awed me into my tame compliance with his eccentricities, when I had feared to ask him to do the slightest incidental thing for me – even though I might know, from his long-continued motionlessness, that behind his screen he must be standing in one of those dead-wall reveries of his.

Revolving all these things, and coupling them with the recently discovered fact that he made my office his constant abiding place and home, and not forgetful of his morbid moodiness; revolving all these things, a prudential feeling began to steal over me. My first emotions had been those of pure melancholy and sincerest pity; but just in proportion as the forlornness of Bartleby grew and grew to my imagination, did that same melancholy merge into fear, that pity into repulsion. So true it is, and so terrible too, that up to a certain point the thought or sight of misery enlists our best affections; but, in certain special cases, beyond that point it does not. They err who would assert that invariably this is owing to the inherent selfishness of the human heart. It rather proceeds from a certain hopelessness of remedying excessive and organic ill. To a sensitive being, pity is not seldom pain. And when at last it is perceived that such pity cannot lead to effectual succour, common sense bids the soul be rid of it. What I saw that morning persuaded me that the scrivener was the victim of innate and incurable disorder. I might give alms to his body, but his body did not pain him; it was his soul that suffered, and his soul I could not reach.

I did not accomplish the purpose of going to Trinity Church that morning. Somehow, the things I had seen disqualified me for the time from churchgoing. I walked homeward, thinking what I would do with Bartleby. Finally, I resolved upon this: I would put certain calm questions to him the next morning, touching his history, etc., and if he declined to answer then openly and reservedly (and I supposed he would *prefer not*), then to give him a twenty-dollar bill over and above whatever I might owe him and tell him his services were no longer required; but that if, in any other way, I could assist him, I would be happy to do so, especially if he desired to return to his native place, wherever that might be, I would willingly help to defray the expenses. Moreover, if, after reaching home, he found himself at any time in want of aid, a letter from him would be sure of a reply.

The next morning came.

"Bartleby," said I, gently calling to him behind his screen.

No reply.

"Bartleby," said I, in a still gentler tone, "come here; I am not going to ask you to do anything you would prefer not to do – I simply wish to speak to you."

Upon this, he noiselessly slid into view.

"Will you tell me, Bartleby, where you were born?"

"I would prefer not to."

"Will you tell me anything about yourself?"

"I would prefer not to."

"But what reasonable objection can you have to speak to me? I feel friendly toward you."

He did not look at me while I spoke, but kept his glance fixed upon my bust of Cicero, which, as I then sat, was directly behind me, some six inches above my head.

"What is your answer, Bartleby?" said I, after waiting a considerable time for a reply, during which his countenance remained immovable; only there was the faintest conceivable tremor of the white attenuated mouth.

"At present, I prefer to give no answer," he said, and retired into his hermitage.

It was rather weak in me, I confess, but his manner on this occasion nettled me. Not only did there seem to lurk in it a certain disdain, but his perverseness

HERMAN MELVILLE

seemed ungrateful, considering the undeniable good usage and indulgence he had received from me.

Again I sat ruminating what I should do. Mortified as I was at his behaviour, and resolved as I had been to dismiss him when I entered my office, nevertheless I strangely felt something superstitious knocking at my heart, and forbidding me to carry out my purpose, and denouncing me for a villain if I dared to breathe one bitter word against this forlornest of mankind. At last, familiarly drawing my chair behind his screen, I sat down and said: "Bartleby, never mind, then, about revealing your history; but let me entreat you, as a friend, to comply as far as may be with the usages of this office. Say now you will help to examine papers tomorrow or next day: in short, say now that in a day or two you will begin to be a little reasonable – say so, Bartleby."

"At present, I would prefer not to be a little reasonable," was his mildly cadaverous reply.

Just then the folding doors opened, and Nippers approached. He seemed suffering from an unusually bad night's rest, induced by severer indigestion than common. He overheard those final words of Bartleby.

"Prefer not, eh?" gritted Nippers. "I'd prefer him, if I were you, sir" – addressing me – "I'd prefer him; I'd give him preferences, the stubborn mule! What is it, sir, pray, that he prefers not to do now?"

Bartleby moved not a limb.

"Mr Nippers," said I, "I'd prefer that you would withdraw for the present."

Somehow, of late, I had got into the way of involuntarily using this word *prefer* upon all sorts of not exactly suitable occasions. And I trembled to think that my contact with the scrivener had already and seriously affected me in a mental way. And what further and deeper aberration might it not yet produce? This apprehension had not been without efficacy in determining me to summary means.

As Nippers, looking very sour and sulky, was departing, Turkey blandly and deferentially approached.

"With submission, sir," said he, "yesterday I was thinking about Bartleby here, and I think that if he would but prefer to take a quart of good ale every day, it would do much toward mending him and enabling him to assist in examining his papers."

"So you have got the word too," said I, slightly excited.

"With submission, what word, sir?" asked Turkey, respectfully crowding himself into the contracted space behind the screen, and by so doing, making me jostle the scrivener. "What word, sir?"

"I would prefer to be left alone here," said Bartleby, as if offended at being mobbed in his privacy.

"That's the word, Turkey," said I. "That's it."

"Oh, 'prefer'? Oh, yes – queer word. I never use it myself. But, sir, as I was saying, if he would but *prefer* –"

"Turkey," interrupted I, "you will please withdraw."

"Oh, certainly, sir, if you prefer that I should."

As he opened the folding door to retire, Nippers at his desk caught a glimpse of me, and asked whether I would prefer to have a certain paper copied on blue paper or white. He did not, in the least roguishly, accent the word *prefer*. It was plain that it involuntarily rolled from his tongue. I thought to myself: *Surely I must get rid of a demented man, who already has in some degree turned the tongues, if not the heads, of myself and clerks.* But I thought it prudent not to break the dismission at once.

The next day I noticed that Bartleby did nothing but stand at his window in his dead-wall reverie. Upon asking him why he did not write, he said that he had decided upon doing no more writing.

"Why, how now? what next?" exclaimed I, "do no more writing?"

"No more."

"And what is the reason?"

"Do you not see the reason for yourself," he indifferently replied.

I looked steadfastly at him, and perceived that his eyes looked dull and glazed. Instantly, it occurred to me that his unexampled diligence in copying by his dim window for the first few weeks of his stay with me might have temporarily impaired his vision.

I was touched. I said something in condolence with him. I hinted that, of course, he did wisely in abstaining from writing for a while, and urged him to embrace that opportunity of taking wholesome exercise in the open air. This, however, he did not do. A few days after this, my other clerks being absent, and being in a great hurry to dispatch certain letters by the mail, I thought that, having nothing else earthly to do, Bartleby would surely be less inflexible than usual and carry these letters to the Post Office. But he blankly declined. So, much to my inconvenience, I went myself.

Still added days went by. Whether Bartleby's eyes improved or not, I could not say. To all appearance, I thought they did. But when I asked him if they did, he vouchsafed no answer. At all events, he would do no copying. At last, in reply to my urgings, he informed me that he had permanently given up copying.

"What!" exclaimed I, "suppose your eyes should get entirely well – better than ever before – would you not copy then?"

"I have given up copying," he answered, and slid aside.

He remained as ever, a fixture in my chamber. Nay – if that were possible – he became still more of a fixture than before. What was to be done? He would do nothing in the office; why should he stay there? In plain fact, he had now become a millstone to me, not only useless as a necklace, but afflictive to bear. Yet I was sorry for him. I speak less than truth when I say that, on his own account, he occasioned me uneasiness. If he would but have named a single relative or friend, I would instantly have written and urged their taking the poor fellow away to some convenient retreat. But he seemed alone, absolutely alone in the universe. A bit of wreck in the mid-Atlantic. At length, necessities connected with my business tyrannized over all other considerations. Decently as I could, I told Bartleby that in six days' time he must unconditionally leave the office. I warned him to take measures, in the interval, for procuring some other abode. I offered to assist him in this endeavour, if he himself would but take the first step toward a removal. "And when you finally quit me, Bartleby," added I, "I shall see that you go not away entirely unprovided. Six days from this hour, remember."

At the expiration of that period, I peeped behind the screen and lo! Bartleby was there.

I buttoned up my coat, balanced myself; advanced slowly toward him, touched his shoulder, and said, "The time has come; you must quit this place; I am sorry for you; here is money. But you must go."

"I would prefer not," he replied, with his back still toward me.

"You must."

He remained silent.

Now I had an unbounded confidence in this man's common honesty. He had frequently restored to me sixpences and shillings carelessly dropped upon the floor, for I am apt to be very reckless in such shirt-button affairs. The proceeding then which followed will not be deemed extraordinary.

"Bartleby," said I, "I owe you twelve dollars on account. Here are thirty-two; the odd twenty are yours. Will you take it?" And I handed the bills toward him.

But he made no motion.

"I will leave them here, then," I said, putting them under a weight on the table. Then, taking my hat and cane and going to the door, I tranquilly turned and added: "After you have removed your things from these offices, Bartleby, you will of course lock the door, since everyone is now gone for the day but you; and, if you please, slip your key underneath the mat so that I may have it in the morning. I shall not see you again; so goodbye to you. If hereafter in your new place of abode I can be of any service to you, do not fail to advise me by letter. Goodbye, Bartleby, and fare you well."

But he answered not a word; like the last column of some ruined temple, he remained standing mute and solitary in the middle of the otherwise deserted room.

As I walked home in a pensive mood, my vanity got the better of my pity. I could not but highly plume myself on my masterly management in getting rid of Bartleby. 'Masterly', I call it, and such it must appear to any dispassionate thinker. The beauty of my procedure seemed to consist in its perfect quietness. There was no vulgar bullying, no bravado of any sort, no choleric hectoring and striding to and fro across the apartment, jerking out vehement commands for Bartleby to bundle himself off with his beggarly traps. Nothing of the kind. Without loudly bidding Bartleby depart – as an inferior genius might have done – I assumed the ground that depart he must; and upon the assumption built all I had to say. The more I thought over my procedure, the more I was charmed with it.

Nevertheless, next morning, upon awakening, I had my doubts; I had somehow slept off the fumes of vanity. One of the coolest and wisest hours a man has is just after he awakes in the morning. My procedure seemed as sagacious as ever – but only in theory. How it would prove in practice? There was the rub. It was truly a beautiful thought to have assumed Bartleby's departure; but, after all, that assumption was simply my own, and none of Bartleby's. The great point was not whether I had assumed that he would quit me, but whether he would *prefer* so to do. He was more a man of preferences than assumptions.

After breakfast, I walked downtown, arguing the probabilities pro and con. One moment I thought it would prove a miserable failure, and Bartleby would be found all alive at my office as usual; the next moment it seemed certain that I should see his chair empty. And so I kept veering about. At the corner of Broadway and Canal Street, I saw quite an excited group of people standing in earnest conversation.

"I'll take odds he doesn't," said a voice as I passed.

"Doesn't go? Done!" said I, "put up your money."

I was instinctively putting my hand in my pocket

to produce my own, when I remembered that this was an election day. The words I had overheard bore no reference to Bartleby, but to the success or non-success of some candidate for the mayoralty. In my intent frame of mind, I had, as it were, imagined that all Broadway shared in my excitement, and were debating the same question with me. I passed on, very thankful that the uproar of the street screened my momentary absent-mindedness.

As I had intended, I was earlier than usual at my office door. I stood listening for a moment. All was still. He must be gone. I tried the knob. The door was locked. Yes, my procedure had worked to a charm; he indeed must be vanished. Yet a certain melancholy mixed with this: I was almost sorry for my brilliant success. I was fumbling under the doormat for the key, which Bartleby was to have left there for me, when accidentally my knee knocked against a panel, producing a summoning sound, and in response a voice came to me from within: "Not yet; I am occupied."

It was Bartleby.

I was thunderstruck. For an instant, I stood like the man who, pipe in mouth, was killed one cloudless afternoon long ago in Virginia by summer lightning; at his own warm open window he was killed, and remained leaning out there upon the dreamy afternoon, till some one touched him, when he fell.

"Not gone!" I murmured at last. But again obeying that wondrous ascendancy which the inscrutable scrivener had over me, and from which ascendancy, for all my chafing, I could not completely escape, I slowly went downstairs and out into the street, and, while walking round the block, considered what I should next do in this unheard-of perplexity. Turn the man out by an actual thrusting, I could not; to drive him away by calling him hard names would not do; calling in the police was an unpleasant idea; and yet, permit him to enjoy his cadaverous triumph over me? This, too, I could not think of. What was to be done? Or, if nothing could be done, was there anything further that I could assume in the matter? Yes, as before I had prospectively assumed that Bartleby would depart, so now I might retrospectively assume that departed he was. In the legitimate carrying out of this assumption, I might enter my office in a great hurry, and, pretending not to see Bartleby at all, walk straight against him as if he were air. Such a proceeding would in a singular degree have the appearance of a home-thrust. It was hardly possible that Bartleby could withstand such an application of the doctrine of assumptions. But upon

HERMAN MELVILLE

second thoughts, the success of the plan seemed rather dubious. I resolved to argue the matter over with him again.

"Bartleby," said I, entering the office, with a quietly severe expression, "I am seriously displeased. I am pained, Bartleby. I had thought better of you. I had imagined you of such a gentlemanly organization that in any delicate dilemma a slight hint would suffice – in short, an assumption. But it appears I am deceived. Why," I added, unaffectedly starting, "you have not even touched the money yet." I pointed to it, just where I had left it the evening previous.

He answered nothing.

"Will you, or will you not, quit me?" I now demanded in a sudden passion, advancing close to him.

"I would prefer not to quit you," he replied, gently emphasizing the "not".

"What earthly right have you to stay here? Do you pay any rent? Do you pay my taxes? Or is this property yours?"

He answered nothing.

"Are you ready to go on and write now? Are your eyes recovered? Could you copy a small paper for me this morning? Or help examine a few lines? Or step round to the Post Office? In a word, will you do anything at

50

all, to give a colouring to your refusal to depart the premises?"

He silently retired into his hermitage.

I was now in such a state of nervous resentment that I thought it but prudent to check myself at present from further demonstrations. Bartleby and I were alone. I remembered the tragedy of the unfortunate Adams and the still more unfortunate Colt in the solitary office of the latter; and how poor Colt, being dreadfully incensed by Adams, and imprudently permitting himself to get wildly excited, was at unawares hurried into his fatal act – an act which certainly no man could possibly deplore more than the actor himself. Often, it had occurred to me in my ponderings upon the subject that had that altercation taken place in the public street, or at a private residence, it would not have terminated as it did. It was the circumstance of being alone in a solitary office, upstairs, of a building entirely unhallowed by humanizing domestic associations – an uncarpeted office, doubtless, of a dusty, haggard sort of appearance; this it must have been, which greatly helped to enhance the irritable desperation of the hapless Colt.

But when this old Adam of resentment rose in me and tempted me concerning Bartleby, I grappled

HERMAN MELVILLE

him and threw him. How? Why, simply by recalling the divine injunction: "A new commandment give I unto you, that ye love one another." Yes, this it was that saved me. Aside from higher considerations, charity often operates as a vastly wise and prudent principle, a great safeguard to its possessor. Men have committed murder for jealousy's sake, and anger's sake, and hatred's sake, and selfishness's sake, and spiritual pride's sake; but no man that ever I heard of ever committed a diabolical murder for sweet charity's sake. Mere self-interest, then, if no better motive can be enlisted, should, especially with high-tempered men, prompt all beings to charity and philanthropy. At any rate, upon the occasion in question, I strove to drown my exasperated feelings toward the scrivener by benevolently construing his conduct. *Poor fellow ... poor fellow!* thought I, *he don't mean anything; and besides, he has seen hard times, and ought to be indulged.*

I endeavoured also immediately to occupy myself, and at the same time to comfort my despondency. I tried to fancy that, in the course of the morning, at such time as might prove agreeable to him, Bartleby, of his own free accord, would emerge from his hermitage and take up some decided line of march in the direction of the door. But no. Half-past twelve o'clock came; Turkey began to glow in the face, overturn his inkstand and become generally obstreperous; Nippers abated down into quietude and courtesy; Ginger Nut munched his noon apple; and Bartleby remained standing at his window in one of his profoundest dead-wall reveries. Will it be credited? Ought I to acknowledge it? That afternoon I left the office without saying one further word to him.

Some days now passed, during which, at leisure intervals, I looked a little into *Edwards on the Will*, and *Priestley on Necessity*. Under the circumstances, those books induced a salutary feeling. Gradually, I slid into the persuasion that these troubles of mine touching the scrivener had been all predestined from eternity, and Bartleby was billeted upon me for some mysterious purpose of an all-wise Providence, which it was not for a mere mortal like me to fathom. *Yes, Bartleby, stay there behind your screen,* thought I, *I shall persecute you no more; you are harmless and noiseless as any of these old chairs; in short, I never feel so private as when I know you are here. At least I see it, I feel it; I penetrate to the predestinated purpose of my life. I am content. Others may have loftier parts to enact; but my mission in this world, Bartleby, is to furnish you with office-*

room for such period as you may see fit to remain.

I believe that this wise and blessed frame of mind would have continued with me, had it not been for the unsolicited and uncharitable remarks obtruded upon me by my professional friends who visited the rooms. But thus it often is, that the constant friction of illiberal minds wears out, at last, the best resolves of the more generous. Though to be sure, when I reflected upon it, it was not strange that people entering my office should be struck by the peculiar aspect of the unaccountable Bartleby, and so be tempted to throw out some sinister observations concerning him. Sometimes an attorney having business with me, and calling at my office, and finding no one but the scrivener there, would undertake to obtain some sort of precise information from him touching my whereabouts; but without heeding his idle talk, Bartleby would remain standing immovable in the middle of the room. So after contemplating him in that position for a time, the attorney would depart, no wiser than he came.

Also, when a Reference was going on, and the room full of lawyers and witnesses and business was driving fast, some deeply occupied legal gentleman present, seeing Bartleby wholly unemployed, would request him to run round to his (the legal gentleman's) office and fetch some papers for him. Thereupon Bartleby would tranquilly decline, and yet remain idle as before. Then the lawyer would give a great stare, and turn to me. And what could I say? At last, I was made aware that all through the circle of my professional acquaintance, a whisper of wonder was running round, having reference to the strange creature I kept at my office. This worried me very much. And as the idea came upon me of his possibly turning out a long-lived man and continuing to occupy my chambers; and denying my authority; and perplexing my visitors; and scandalizing my professional reputation; and casting a general gloom over the premises; and keeping soul and body together to the last upon his savings (for doubtless he spent but half a dime a day), and in the end perhaps outlive me, and claim possession of my office by right of his perpetual occupancy: as all these dark anticipations crowded upon me more and more, and my friends continually intruded their relentless remarks upon the apparition in my room, a great change was wrought in me. I resolved to gather all my faculties together, and forever rid me of this intolerable incubus.

Ere revolving any complicated project, however, adapted to this end, I first simply suggested to Bartleby the propriety of his permanent departure. In a calm and serious tone, I commended the idea to his careful and mature consideration. But having taken three days to meditate upon it, he apprised me that his original determination remained the same: in short, that he still preferred to abide with me.

What shall I do? I now said to myself, buttoning up my coat to the last button. *What shall I do? What ought I to do? What does conscience say I should do with this man, or, rather, ghost? Rid myself of him, I must; go, he shall. But how? You will not thrust him, the poor, pale, passive mortal, you will not thrust such a helpless creature out of your door? You will not dishonour yourself by such cruelty? No, I will not, I cannot do that. Rather, would I let him live and die here, and then mason up his remains in the wall. What, then, will you do? For all your coaxing, he will not budge. Bribes he leaves under your own paperweight on your table; in short, it is quite plain that he prefers to cling to you.*

Then something severe, something unusual, must be done. What! Surely you will not have him collared by a constable, and commit his innocent pallor to the common jail? And upon what ground could you procure such a thing to be done? A vagrant, is he? What! He a vagrant, a wanderer, who refuses to budge? It is because he will not be a vagrant, then, that you seek to count him as a vagrant. That is too absurd. No visible means of support: there, I have him. Wrong again: for indubitably he does support himself, and that is the only unanswerable proof that any man can show of his possessing the means so to do. No more, then. Since he will not quit me, I must quit him. I will change my offices; I will move elsewhere and give him fair notice, that if I find him on my new premises I will then proceed against him as a common trespasser.

Acting accordingly, next day I thus addressed him: "I find these chambers too far from the City Hall; the air is unwholesome. In a word, I propose to remove my offices next week, and shall no longer require your services. I tell you this now, in order that you may seek another place."

He made no reply, and nothing more was said.

On the appointed day I engaged carts and men, proceeded to my chambers and, having but little furniture, everything was removed in a few hours. Throughout, the scrivener remained standing behind the screen, which I directed to be removed the last thing. It was withdrawn, and being folded up like a huge folio, left him the motionless occupant of a naked room. I stood in the entry watching him a moment, while something from within me upbraided me.

I re-entered with my hand in my pocket, and ... and my heart in my mouth.

"Goodbye, Bartleby; I am going ... Goodbye, and God some way bless you; and take that" – I slipped something in his hand, but it dropped upon the floor, and then, strange to say, I tore myself from him whom I had so longed to be rid of.

Established in my new quarters, for a day or two I kept the door locked, and started at every footfall in the passages. When I returned to my rooms after any little absence, I would pause at the threshold for an instant, and attentively listen, ere applying my key. But these fears were needless. Bartleby never came nigh me.

I thought all was going well when a perturbed-looking stranger visited me, enquiring whether I was the person who had recently occupied rooms at No. — Wall Street.

Full of forebodings, I replied that I was.

"Then, sir," said the stranger, who proved a lawyer, "you are responsible for the man you left there. He refuses to do any copying; he refuses to do anything; he says he 'prefers not to'; and he refuses to quit the premises."

"I am very sorry, sir," said I, with assumed tranquillity, but an inward tremor, "but, really, the man you allude to is nothing to me – he is no relation or apprentice of mine, that you should hold me responsible for him."

"In mercy's name, who is he?"

"I certainly cannot inform you. I know nothing about him. Formerly I employed him as a copyist; but he has done nothing for me now for some time past."

"I shall settle him then; good morning, sir."

Several days passed, and I heard nothing more; and though I often felt a charitable prompting to call at the place and see poor Bartleby, yet a certain squeamishness of I know not what withheld me.

All is over with him by this time, thought I at last, when through another week no further intelligence reached me. But coming to my room the day after, I found several persons waiting at my door in a high state of nervous excitement.

"That's the man – here he comes," cried the foremost one, whom I recognized as the lawyer who had previously called upon me alone.

"You must take him away, sir, at once," cried a portly person among them, advancing upon me, and whom I knew to be the landlord of No. — Wall Street. "These gentlemen, my tenants, cannot stand it any longer; Mr

B—" – he pointed to the lawyer – "has turned him out of his room, and he now persists in haunting the building generally, sitting upon the banisters of the stairs by day and sleeping in the entry by night. Everybody is concerned. Clients are leaving the offices; some fears are entertained of a mob; something you must do, and that without delay."

Aghast at this torrent, I fell back before it, and would fain have locked myself in my new quarters. In vain, I persisted that Bartleby was nothing to me, no more than to anyone else. In vain: I was the last person known to have anything to do with him, and they held me to terrible account. Fearful then of being exposed in the papers (as one person present obscurely threatened), I considered the matter and, at length, said that if the lawyer would give me a confidential interview with the scrivener, in his (the lawyer's) own room, I would that afternoon strive my best to rid them of the nuisance they complained of.

Going upstairs to my old haunt, there was Bartleby, silently sitting upon the banister at the landing.

"What are you doing here, Bartleby?" said I.

"Sitting upon the banister," he mildly replied.

I motioned him into the lawyer's room, who then left us.

"Bartleby," said I, "are you aware that you are the cause of great tribulation to me, by persisting in occupying the entry after being dismissed from the office?"

No answer.

"Now one of two things must take place. Either you must do something, or something must be done to you. Now what sort of business would you like to engage in? Would you like to re-engage in copying for someone?"

"No; I would prefer not to make any change."

"Would you like a clerkship in a dry-goods store?"

"There is too much confinement about that. No, I would not like a clerkship; but I am not particular."

"'Too much confinement'!" I cried, "why you keep yourself confined all the time!"

"I would prefer not to take a clerkship," he rejoined, as if to settle that little item at once.

"How would a bartender's business suit you? There is no trying of the eyesight in that."

"I would not like it at all; though, as I said before, I am not particular."

His unwonted wordiness inspirited me. I returned to the charge.

"Well, then, would you like to travel through the country collecting bills for the merchants? That would improve your health."

"No, I would prefer to be doing something else."

"How, then, would going as a companion to Europe, to entertain some young gentleman with your conversation, how would that suit you?"

"Not at all. It does not strike me that there is anything definite about that. I like to be stationary. But I am not particular."

"Stationary you shall be then," I cried, now losing all patience, and for the first time in all my exasperating connection with him fairly flying into a passion. "If you do not go away from these premises before night, I shall feel bound – indeed, I am bound – to ... to ... to quit the premises myself!" I rather absurdly concluded, knowing not with what possible threat to try to frighten his immobility into compliance. Despairing of all further efforts, I was precipitately leaving him, when a final thought occurred to me – one that had not been wholly unindulged before.

"Bartleby," said I, in the kindest tone I could assume under such exciting circumstances, "will you go home with me now – not to my office, but my dwelling – and remain there till we can conclude upon some convenient arrangement for you at our leisure? Come, let us start now, right away."

"No; at present, I would prefer not to make any change at all."

I answered nothing, but, effectually dodging everyone by the suddenness and rapidity of my flight, rushed from the building, ran up Wall Street toward Broadway and, jumping into the first omnibus, was soon removed from pursuit. As soon as tranquillity returned, I distinctly perceived that I had now done all that I possibly could, both in respect to the demands of the landlord and his tenants and with regard to my own desire and sense of duty, to benefit Bartleby and shield him from rude persecution. I now strove to be entirely carefree and quiescent; and my conscience justified me in the attempt, though indeed it was not so successful as I could have wished. So fearful was I of being again hunted out by the incensed landlord and his exasperated tenants that, surrendering my business to Nippers, for a few days I drove about the upper part of the town and through the suburbs in my rockaway; crossed over to Jersey City and Hoboken; and paid fugitive visits to Manhattanville and Astoria. In fact, I almost lived in my rockaway for the time.

When again I entered my office, lo, a note from the landlord lay upon the desk. I opened it with trembling hands. It informed me that the writer had sent to the police, and had Bartleby removed to the Tombs as a vagrant. Moreover, since I knew more about him than anyone else, he wished me to appear at that place and make a suitable statement of the facts. These tidings had a conflicting effect upon me. At first, I was indignant; but at last, almost approved. The landlord's energetic, summary disposition had led him to adopt a procedure which I do not think I would have decided upon myself; and yet, as a last resort, under such peculiar circumstances, it seemed the only plan.

As I afterward learned, the poor scrivener, when told that he must be conducted to the Tombs, offered not the slightest obstacle, but – in his pale, unmoving way – silently acquiesced.

Some compassionate and curious bystanders joined the party and, headed by one of the constables arm-in-arm with Bartleby, the silent procession filed its way through all the noise and heat and joy of the roaring thoroughfares at noon.

The same day I received the note, I went to the Tombs or, to speak more properly, the Halls of Justice. Seeking the right officer, I stated the purpose of my call and was informed that the individual I described was indeed within. I then assured the functionary that Bartleby was a perfectly honest man, and greatly to be compassionated, however unaccountably eccentric. I narrated all I knew, and closed by suggesting the idea of letting him remain in as indulgent confinement as possible till something less harsh might be done – though indeed I hardly knew what. At all events, if nothing else could be decided upon, the almshouse must receive him. I then begged to have an interview.

Being under no disgraceful charge, and quite serene and harmless in all his ways, they had permitted him freely to wander about the prison, and especially in the enclosed grass-platted yards thereof. And so I found him there, standing all alone in the quietest of the yards, his face toward a high wall, while all around, from the narrow slits of the jail windows, I thought I saw peering out upon him the eyes of murderers and thieves.

"Bartleby!"

"I know you," he said, without looking round, "and I want nothing to say to you."

"It was not I that brought you here, Bartleby," said I, keenly pained at his implied suspicion. "And to you, this should not be so vile a place. Nothing reproachful attaches to you by being here. And see, it is not so sad a place as one might think. Look, there is the sky, and here is the grass."

"I know where I am," he replied, but would say

nothing more, and so I left him.

As I entered the corridor again, a broad, meat-like man in an apron accosted me. Jerking his thumb over his shoulder, he said: "Is that your friend?"

"Yes."

"Does he want to starve? If he does, let him live on the prison fare, that's all."

"Who are you?" asked I, not knowing what to make of such an unofficially speaking person in such a place.

"I am the grub-man. Such gentlemen as have friends here hire me to provide them with something good to eat."

"Is this so?" said I, turning to the turnkey. He said it was.

"Well, then," said I, slipping some silver into the grub-man's hands. "I want you to give particular attention to my friend there; let him have the best dinner you can get. And you must be as polite to him as possible."

"Introduce me, will you?" said the grub-man, looking at me with an expression that seemed to say he was all impatience for an opportunity to give a specimen of his breeding.

Thinking it would prove of benefit to the scrivener, I acquiesced, and, asking the grub-man his name, went up with him to Bartleby.

"Bartleby, this is Mr Cutlets; you will find him very useful to you."

"Your sarvant, sir, your sarvant," said the grub-man, making a low salutation behind his apron. "Hope you find it pleasant here, sir. Spacious grounds, cool apartments, sir; hope you'll stay with us some time. Try to make it agreeable. May Mrs Cutlets and I have the pleasure of your company to dinner, sir, in Mrs Cutlets's private room?"

"I prefer not to dine today," said Bartleby, turning away. "It would disagree with me; I am unused to dinners." So saying, he slowly moved to the other side of the enclosure and took up a position fronting the dead-wall.

"How's this?" said the grub-man, addressing me with a stare of astonishment. "He's odd, ain't he?"

"I think he is a little deranged," said I, sadly.

"'Deranged'? 'Deranged', is it? Well now, upon my word, I thought that friend of your'n was a gentleman forger; they are always pale and genteel-like, them forgers. I can't help pity 'em – can't help it, sir. Did you know Monroe Edwards?" he added touchingly, and paused. Then, laying his hand pityingly on my shoulder, he sighed: "He died of consumption at Sing

Sing. So you weren't acquainted with Monroe?"

"No, I was never socially acquainted with any forgers. But I cannot stop longer. Look to my friend yonder. You will not lose by it. I will see you again."

Some few days after this, I again obtained admission to the Tombs and went through the corridors in quest of Bartleby – but without finding him.

"I saw him coming from his cell not long ago," said a turnkey, "maybe he's gone to loiter in the yards."

So I went in that direction.

"Are you looking for the silent man?" said another turnkey, passing me. "Yonder he lies – sleeping in the yard there. 'Tis not twenty minutes since I saw him lie down."

The yard was entirely quiet. It was not accessible to the common prisoners. The surrounding walls, of amazing thickness, kept off all sounds behind them. The Egyptian character of the masonry weighed upon me with its gloom. But a soft imprisoned turf grew underfoot. The heart of the eternal pyramids, it seemed, wherein, by some strange magic, through the clefts, grass-seed dropped by birds had sprung.

Strangely huddled at the base of the wall, his knees drawn up, and lying on his side, his head touching the cold stones, I saw the wasted Bartleby. But nothing stirred. I paused, then went close up to him, stooped over and saw that his dim eyes were open; otherwise, he seemed profoundly sleeping. Something prompted me to touch him. I felt his hand, when a tingling shiver ran up my arm and down my spine to my feet.

The round face of the grub-man peered upon me now. "His dinner is ready. Won't he dine today, either? Or does he live without dining?"

"Lives without dining," said I, and closed the eyes.

"Eh! He's asleep, ain't he?"

"With kings and counsellors," murmured I.

There would seem little need for proceeding further in this history. Imagination will readily supply the meagre recital of poor Bartleby's interment. But ere parting with the reader, let me say, that if this little narrative has sufficiently interested him to awaken curiosity as to who Bartleby was, and what manner of life he led prior to the present narrator's making his acquaintance, I can only reply that in such curiosity I fully share – but am wholly unable to gratify it. Yet here I hardly know whether I should divulge one little item of rumour, which came to my ear a few months after the scrivener's decease. Upon what basis it rested, I could never ascertain; and hence, how true it is, I cannot now tell. But inasmuch as this vague report has not been without a certain strange suggestive interest to me, however sad, it may prove the same with some others; and so I will briefly mention it.

The report was this: that Bartleby had been a subordinate clerk in the Dead Letter Office in Washington, from which he had been suddenly removed by a change in the administration. When I think over this rumour, I cannot adequately express the emotions that seize me. Dead letters! Does it not sound like 'dead men'? Conceive a man by nature and misfortune, prone to a pallid hopelessness; can any business seem more fitted to heighten it than that of continually handling these dead letters and assorting them for the flames? For by the cartload, they are annually burned. Sometimes from out the folded paper the pale clerk takes a ring: the finger it was meant for, perhaps, moulders in the grave. A banknote sent in swiftest charity: he whom it would relieve, nor eats nor hungers anymore; pardon for those who died despairing; hope for those who died unhoping; good tidings for those who died stifled by unrelieved calamities. On errands of life, these letters speed to death.

Ah, Bartleby! Ah, humanity!

Other titles from Paper + Ink

Rūdolfs Blaumanis
In the Shadow of Death
Translated from the Latvian by Uldis Balodis

Mehis Heinsaar
The Butterfly Man & Other Stories
Translated from the Estonian by Tiina Randviir and Adam Cullen

O. Henry
The Gift of the Magi & Other Stories

D. H. Lawrence
The Rocking Horse Winner & Other Stories

Katherine Mansfield
The Garden Party & Other Stories

Guy de Maupassant
The Necklace & Other Stories

Mark Twain
*The Celebrated Jumping Frog of Calaveras County
& Other Stories*

Vazha-Pshavela
The Death of Bagrat Zakharych & Other Stories
Translated from the Georgian by Rebecca Ruth Gould

Oscar Wilde
The Happy Prince & Other Stories

Žemaitė
Tofylis, or the Marriage of Zosė
Translated from the Lithuanian by Violeta Kelertas

Visit **www.paperand.ink** to subscribe and receive books by post, as well as
to keep up to date about new volumes in the series.